The Power of Visualization Harnessing Your Imagination to Manifest Success

Shumaila Imtiaz

pencil

ISBN 978-93-5883-116-0
© Shumaila Imtiaz 2023

Published in India 2023 by Pencil

A brand of
One Point Six Technologies Pvt. Ltd.
Unit no. 26, Ground Floor, Building A1,
Wadala Truck Terminal Road,
Near Post Office, Antop Hill, Mumbai - 400037
E connect@thepencilapp.com
W www.thepencilapp.com

DISCLAIMER: *The opinions expressed in this book are those of the authors and do not purport to reflect the views of the Publisher.*

Author biography

Shumaila Imtiaz is a highly acclaimed wellness coach and author, whose exceptional work in the field of self-love and leadership has left an indelible mark on countless lives. With a profound understanding of human behavior and a genuine passion for empowering others, she has dedicated her career to guiding individuals towards holistic well-being and personal growth. Through her transformative coaching programs, Shumaila fosters a safe and compassionate space for clients to explore their inner selves, embrace their worthiness, and overcome self-doubt. As an accomplished author, her books serve as powerful tools for readers seeking to cultivate self-love, develop authentic leadership skills, and create meaningful connections with others. Her writing style, coupled with practical exercises and relatable anecdotes, resonates deeply with audiences, igniting a sense of empowerment and inspiring positive change. The impact of her work extends far beyond accolades, as Shumaila continues to be a beacon of hope and wisdom, encouraging individuals to embark on transformative journeys of self-discovery and personal empowerment. Through her unwavering commitment to spreading messages of self-love and leadership, Shumaila leaves a lasting legacy of compassion, resilience, and positive transformation.

CONTENTS

The Power of Visualization

The Power of Visualization: Harnessing Your Imagination to Manifest Success

Welcome to "The Power of Visualization: Harnessing Your Imagination to Manifest Success." In this eBook, we will explore the incredible potential of visualization as a transformative tool to achieve your goals, enhance your performance, and create a life filled with purpose and abundance. Visualization is a mental technique that involves using your imagination to create vivid mental images of your desired outcomes. By engaging your senses and emotions in this process, you can align your thoughts, beliefs, and actions with your aspirations, paving the way for tangible results. Let's embark on this journey to discover the extraordinary power that visualization holds and how you can integrate it into your daily life for profound personal growth.

Chapter 1

Understanding Visualization- What is visualization and how does it work?

In this introductory chapter, we delve into the concept of visualization and its underlying principles. We explore the idea that thoughts have a significant impact on our reality and how visualization works to bridge the gap between imagination and tangible results. The chapter discusses the scientific evidence supporting the effectiveness of visualization, highlighting how it influences the brain's neural pathways and influences our actions. Additionally, we explore various visualization techniques, including guided visualization, mental rehearsal, and creative visualization, and their applications in different areas of life. The science behind visualization: the link between the mind and reality- Different types of visualization techniques and their applications- The role of the subconscious mind in visualization

Understanding Visualization: A Comprehensive Exploration of Its Mechanisms and Impact

Visualization, often referred to as mental imagery or mental rehearsal, is a powerful cognitive technique that involves creating vivid mental images of desired outcomes or scenarios. By engaging the mind's eye and senses, individuals can harness the potential of visualization to influence their thoughts, emotions, and behaviors. This report aims to provide a detailed understanding of visualization, exploring its underlying mechanisms, scientific evidence supporting its efficacy, and its diverse applications in various aspects of life.

The Mechanisms of Visualization: At the core of visualization lies the interplay between the conscious and subconscious mind. When we visualize, we activate the same neural pathways in the brain as when we physically experience the imagined scenario. This process establishes new mental connections and reinforces existing ones, shaping our beliefs, attitudes, and actions. Moreover, visualization engages the brain's reticular activating system (RAS), which filters information and directs our attention. By visualizing specific goals, we prime the RAS to notice relevant opportunities and resources in our external environment, aligning our focus with our aspirations.

The Science behind Visualization: Numerous scientific studies have validated the effectiveness of visualization. Brain imaging studies have shown that mental rehearsal activates the same brain regions as real experiences. For instance, visualizing a physical movement triggers the activation of motor-related brain areas. These findings demonstrate the tangible impact of visualization on brain functioning and support its potential to improve performance in sports, art, and other skills.

Applications of Visualization: 1. Sports Performance: Athletes use visualization to mentally rehearse their performances, enhancing their skills, boosting confidence, and reducing anxiety. Studies have shown that athletes who visualize their success tend to exhibit improved performance on the field.

2. Personal Development: Visualization plays a vital role in setting and achieving goals. By creating detailed mental images of desired outcomes, individuals build a strong connection between their aspirations and actions, increasing their motivation and commitment to success.

3. Overcoming Fears and Phobias: Exposure visualization is an effective technique for confronting fears and phobias. By repeatedly visualizing themselves facing their fears,

individuals can reduce anxiety and gradually build resilience.

4. Health and Healing: Visualization has been employed as a complementary therapy for physical and emotional healing. By visualizing optimal health and wellness, individuals can positively influence their immune system and overall well-being.

5. Creativity and Problem-Solving: Visualizing creative ideas and potential solutions to challenges can stimulate innovation and foster breakthrough thinking.

Practical Techniques for Effective Visualization: 1. Relaxation and Mindfulness: Before visualizing, it is crucial to create a relaxed and focused mental space. Practicing deep breathing and mindfulness techniques can calm the mind and prepare it for visualization.

2. Sensory Details and Emotions: Incorporating sensory details (sights, sounds, smells, tastes, and feelings) in visualizations makes them more vivid and powerful. Engaging emotions during visualization enhances the emotional connection to the desired outcomes.

3. Affirmations and Positive Self-talk: Using affirmations and positive self-talk helps reinforce belief in the effectiveness of visualization, supporting one's confidence in achieving their goals.

As we continue to explore the depths of visualization, it becomes evident that this mental practice holds the key to unlocking our full potential and manifesting the life we desire.

Chapter 2

Setting Clear Intentions- Before embarking on any visualization practice, it is crucial to set clear intentions and define your goals. This chapter focuses on the importance of setting specific, measurable, achievable, relevant, and time-bound (SMART) goals that align with your deepest desires and values. It guides readers through self-reflection exercises to identify their true intentions and teaches them how to use these intentions as the foundation for their visualization practice. The chapter also introduces the concept of a vision board and how it can be used to visualize goals and dreams effectively. The importance of setting specific, measurable, achievable, relevant, and time-bound (SMART) goals- Identifying your deepest desires and intentions- How to align your intentions with your values and beliefs- Creating a vision board to visualize your goals and dreams

The Foundation for Achieving Your Goals and Aspirations:

Setting clear intentions is a fundamental step in the process of achieving our goals and aspirations. Intentions act as a guiding force that directs our focus, thoughts, and actions towards the desired outcome. In this report, we will delve into the importance of setting clear intentions, the benefits they offer, and practical strategies for crafting effective intentions that align with our values and aspirations.

The Significance of Setting Clear Intentions:

Clear intentions provide clarity and purpose, serving as a roadmap for our journey towards success. When we set specific intentions, we define what we want to achieve and why it matters to us. This clarity eliminates ambiguity, enhances motivation, and empowers us to take decisive actions. Clear intentions also activate the reticular activating system (RAS) in our brain, making us more attentive to relevant opportunities and resources in our environment that can support our goals.

The Power of Specificity in Intentions:

Specificity in intentions is crucial as it paints a detailed picture of the desired outcome. Vague intentions lack direction and may lead to aimless pursuits. Specific intentions, on the other hand, define the who, what, when, where, and why of our objectives. By setting specific intentions, we make it easier to measure progress and identify the necessary steps to achieve our goals.

Aligning Intentions with Values and Aspirations:

For intentions to be effective, they must align with our core values and long-term aspirations. When intentions resonate with our values, they become deeply meaningful and inspiring, motivating us to stay committed even in the face of challenges. Aligning intentions with our aspirations ensures that they contribute to our overall vision of success and fulfillment.

Crafting Effective Intentions:

1. Start with Self-Reflection: Begin by reflecting on your values, passions, and long-term aspirations. Consider what truly matters to you and what you want to achieve in

various aspects of your life, such as career, relationships, health, and personal growth.

2. Use the SMART Criteria: Employ the SMART criteria (Specific, Measurable, Achievable, Relevant, and Time-bound) to structure your intentions effectively. Ensure that each intention is clear, quantifiable, realistic, relevant to your goals, and set within a specific timeframe.

3. Be Positive and Present Tense: Frame your intentions in positive language and present tense to affirm that you are already moving towards your desired outcome. For example, "I am confidently expressing myself in public speaking" rather than "I will overcome my fear of public speaking."

4. Visualize the Outcome: Visualize yourself achieving the intended outcome. Engage your senses and emotions in this mental imagery to create a powerful connection with your intentions.

5. Write down Your Intentions: Putting your intentions in writing solidifies your commitment to them. Use a journal or vision board to record your intentions and refer to them regularly for reinforcement.

Benefits of Setting Clear Intentions:

1. Enhanced Focus and Motivation: Clear intentions provide a focal point for your efforts, keeping you motivated and on track.

2. Improved Decision-Making: When you know what you want to achieve, decision-making becomes more

straightforward, as you can assess options based on how well they align with your intentions.

3. Increased Resilience: Clear intentions provide a sense of purpose, empowering you to overcome obstacles and setbacks with greater resilience.

4. Heightened Self-Awareness: Setting intentions involves introspection, leading to increased self-awareness and personal growth.

As we continue to set clear intentions and pursue our dreams with determination, we empower ourselves to create a life filled with purpose, fulfillment, and accomplishment.

Chapter 3: Crafting the Perfect Visualization Practice- Designing a conducive environment for visualization- Mastering relaxation and mindfulness techniques to enhance visualization- Tips for effectively using affirmations and positive self-talk during the process- The art of scripting: writing your success story in detail. To make the most of visualization, one must create an optimal practice environment. This chapter discusses the importance of relaxation and mindfulness techniques to prepare the mind for visualization. It provides step-by-step guidance on mastering relaxation exercises, breathing techniques, and creating a peaceful and focused mental space for visualization. Additionally, readers learn how to incorporate affirmations and positive self-talk during the process to reinforce their belief in the effectiveness of visualization. The chapter concludes with tips on scripting – the act of writing down the details of one's success story

– to enhance the visualization experience. Cultivating a Powerful Mental Tool for Personal Growth and Achievement.

Visualization, also known as mental imagery, is a potent mental practice that can significantly impact our thoughts, emotions, and actions. Crafting the perfect visualization practice involves creating a conducive environment and employing effective techniques to enhance the power and efficacy of this transformative tool. In this report, we will explore the key elements of a successful visualization practice and provide practical strategies for harnessing the full potential of visualization in various aspects of life.

Designing a Conducive Environment for Visualization:

1. Choose a Quiet and Comfortable Space: Find a peaceful environment where you can be free from distractions and interruptions. Whether it's a quiet room in your home or a serene outdoor location, the goal is to create an atmosphere that promotes relaxation and focus.

2. Eliminate Digital Distractions: Turn off electronic devices and notifications to prevent any interruptions during your visualization sessions. This will allow you to fully immerse yourself in the experience.

3. Set an Appropriate Time: Select a time when you are naturally alert and receptive to visualization. For many people, early mornings or before bedtime are ideal for visualization practice.

Mastering Relaxation and Mindfulness Techniques:

1. Deep Breathing Exercises: Begin each visualization session with deep, slow breaths to relax your body and mind. Deep breathing calms the nervous system and prepares you for a more profound visualization experience.

2. Progressive Muscle Relaxation: Progressively tense and release different muscle groups to release physical tension and achieve a state of deep relaxation.

3. Mindfulness Meditation: Practice mindfulness to cultivate present-moment awareness and reduce mental chatter. Mindfulness can improve focus during visualization and increase your receptivity to positive suggestions.

Tips for Effectively Using Affirmations and Positive Self-talk:

1. Frame Affirmations Positively: Craft affirmations in a positive and present tense manner. For instance, instead of saying, "I will overcome challenges," say, "I overcome challenges with ease and confidence."

2. Make Affirmations Personal: Tailor affirmations to reflect your individual goals and aspirations. Personalized affirmations have a more profound impact on the subconscious mind.

3. Repeat Affirmations with Conviction: Speak your affirmations with confidence and conviction. Believing in the truth of your affirmations reinforces their effectiveness.

The Art of Scripting: Writing Your Success Story in Detail:

1. Describe the Desired Outcome: Write a detailed description of your desired outcome or goal. Use sensory language to vividly portray how it feels, looks, and sounds when you achieve your objective.

2. Include Emotions and Feelings: Describe the emotions and feelings associated with your success. Engaging emotions in your visualization makes the experience more potent and inspiring.

3. Visualize the Journey: Write about the steps and actions you take to achieve your goal. Visualizing the journey helps you identify potential obstacles and plan strategies for overcoming them.

Applications of Visualization Techniques:

1. Goal Achievement: Use visualization to visualize the successful attainment of your goals, making the process more tangible and achievable.

2. Performance Enhancement: Athletes, artists, and professionals can use visualization to mentally rehearse their performances, enhancing skills and confidence.

3. Overcoming Challenges: Visualization can help you confront fears and challenges, increasing resilience and self-assurance.

As you continue to refine your visualization practice, you will unlock the potential to create a more positive and empowered life, filled with endless possibilities and opportunities for success.

Chapter 4: Visualizing Your Ideal Self and Life- Step-by-step guide to visualizing your ideal self and life- It delves deeper into the core of visualization: visualizing one's ideal self and life. It provides a systematic guide on how to engage all the senses and emotions during the visualization process to amplify its impact. Readers learn to create vivid mental images of their desired outcomes, focusing on sensory details like sights, sounds, smells, tastes, and feelings to make the visualizations more real and powerful. Moreover, the chapter addresses common challenges such as self-doubt and skepticism that may arise during visualization and offers strategies to overcome them. It also emphasizes the role of gratitude in elevating the effectiveness of visualization. Enhancing clarity through sensory details and emotions- How to overcome self-doubt and skepticism during the visualization process- The role of gratitude in amplifying the power of visualization.

It is a Transformative Journey towards Personal Fulfillment and Success

Visualizing your ideal self and life is a powerful practice that allows you to create a compelling mental image of the person you aspire to be and the life you want to live. By engaging your imagination and emotions, you can align your thoughts and actions with your deepest desires, making your dreams a tangible reality. This report explores the process of visualizing your ideal self and life, the benefits it offers, and practical strategies to optimize its impact.

The Process of Visualizing Your Ideal Self and Life:

1. Cultivate Self-Awareness: Begin by cultivating self-awareness to gain clarity about your values, passions, and aspirations. Reflect on the aspects of your life that bring you joy and fulfillment, and envision the person you want to become.

2. Engage the Senses: To make your visualizations more potent, engage all your senses in the process. Envision not only how your ideal self and life look, but also how they feel, sound, smell, and even taste. Sensory engagement deepens your connection to the visualization, making it more vivid and compelling.

3. Embrace Emotional Connection: Allow yourself to feel the emotions associated with living your ideal life and embodying your ideal self. Emotions are a powerful driving force that can energize your intentions and propel you towards your goals.

4. Create a Clear Mental Picture: Be specific and detailed in your visualization. Imagine the specific attributes and qualities of your ideal self, along with the experiences and accomplishments that define your ideal life.

Benefits of Visualizing Your Ideal Self and Life:

1. Enhanced Clarity and Focus: Visualizing your ideal self and life provides clarity about your aspirations and goals. This clarity empowers you to set clear intentions and make decisions that align with your vision.

2. Increased Motivation and Confidence: As you vividly visualize yourself living your ideal life, you naturally feel motivated to take action. The emotional connection to your visualization fosters a sense of confidence in your abilities to achieve your goals.

3. Overcoming Limiting Beliefs: Visualization can help you identify and overcome limiting beliefs that may be holding you back from realizing your full potential. By envisioning a life beyond self-imposed limitations, you expand your belief in what is possible.

4. Positive Mindset and Resilience: Visualizing your ideal self and life nurtures a positive mindset, which in turn enhances your resilience in the face of challenges and setbacks. A positive outlook helps you navigate obstacles with determination and perseverance.

Practical Strategies for Visualizing Your Ideal Self and Life:

1. Daily Visualization Practice: Set aside dedicated time each day for visualization. Consistency is key to strengthening the neural pathways associated with your ideal self and life.

2. Visualization Rituals: Create visualization rituals that help you get into a focused and relaxed state. Incorporate deep breathing exercises, mindfulness practices, or calming music to set the ambiance for your visualization sessions.

3. Vision Boards: Design a vision board that visually represents your ideal self and life. Include images, quotes, and symbols that resonate with your aspirations. Place the

vision board in a prominent location to remind yourself daily of your goals.

4. Guided Visualization: Utilize guided visualization resources, such as recorded audio sessions or meditation apps, to guide your visualization practice effectively.

Visualization provides a powerful roadmap to guide you on your journey towards becoming the best version of yourself and living a life of purpose and achievement. As you continue to nurture your visualization practice, you will find yourself empowered to take decisive steps towards your goals, leading to a more fulfilling and meaningful life.

Chapter 5: Leveraging Visualization for Peak Performance- Visualization for athletes and sports professionals: improving skills and achieving peak performance- Enhancing creativity and problem-solving abilities through visualization- Visualization as a tool for public speaking and performance anxiety- Boosting academic and professional performance through mental rehearsals Visualization is a potent tool for enhancing performance in various fields. In this chapter, we explore how athletes and sports professionals can use visualization to improve skills and achieve peak performance. Readers learn how to mentally rehearse scenarios, visualize successful performances, and build mental resilience for competitions.

Unleash Your Full Potential in Sports, Arts, and Professional Endeavors. Visualization is a powerful mental technique used by athletes, artists, and professionals to enhance their performance and achieve peak results. By vividly imagining successful outcomes, individuals can create mental rehearsals that prime their minds and bodies for success. This report explores the concept of leveraging visualization for peak performance, the science behind its effectiveness, and practical strategies for optimizing its impact in various domains.

Understanding the Science of Visualization for Peak Performance:

Visualization operates on the principle of the brain's ability to create and strengthen neural connections between mental images and physical actions. When an individual visualizes themselves performing a specific task or activity, the same neural pathways are activated as when they physically engage in that task. These repeated mental rehearsals essentially train the brain and muscles, improving muscle memory, focus, and overall performance.

Benefits of Visualization for Peak Performance:

1. Improved Confidence and Self-Belief: Visualization instills a deep sense of confidence by allowing individuals to witness themselves succeeding repeatedly in their minds. This self-belief translates into increased assertiveness and composure during actual performance.

2. Enhanced Skill Acquisition: When visualizing the execution of specific skills, individuals refine their techniques, correct errors, and visualize the perfect execution. As a result, the brain becomes better equipped

to translate those mental images into refined physical actions.

3. Reduced Performance Anxiety: By rehearsing success mentally, individuals learn to manage performance anxiety effectively. Visualization helps them anticipate and cope with nerves, leading to calmer and more focused performances.

4. Greater Resilience: Visualization aids in building resilience by mentally preparing individuals for setbacks and challenges. When individuals visualize themselves overcoming obstacles, they cultivate a mindset of determination and adaptability.

Strategies for Leveraging Visualization for Peak Performance:

1. Create Detailed Mental Representations: Visualize the desired performance in great detail, incorporating sensory information, such as sights, sounds, and sensations. For athletes, this might involve imagining the texture of the playing surface or the cheering crowd.

2. Visualize Both Success and Obstacles: In addition to envisioning successful outcomes, visualize potential obstacles and how you will navigate them. By mentally preparing for challenges, you increase your ability to respond effectively in real-life situations.

3. Engage Emotions in Visualization: Incorporate positive emotions, such as joy, excitement, and triumph, into your mental rehearsals. Emotions add depth to the visualization, making it more engaging and impactful.

4. Practice Consistently: Regular and consistent visualization practice is key to optimizing its benefits. Set aside dedicated time each day to engage in focused visualization sessions.

5. Complement Visualization with Physical Practice: Visualization works best when combined with physical practice. Use visualization as a supplemental tool to reinforce the skills and techniques practiced in real-life scenarios.

Applications of Visualization for Peak Performance:

1. Sports Performance: Athletes can visualize themselves executing plays, making successful shots, or crossing the finish line first. Golfers, in particular, use visualization to imagine the perfect swing and visualize the ball's track.

2. Performing Arts: Musicians, actors, and dancers use visualization to mentally rehearse their performances, ensuring they deliver flawless and expressive presentations.

3. Professional Success: Business professionals can employ visualization techniques for public speaking, negotiations, and challenging meetings, preparing themselves for successful outcomes.

Through consistent practice and detailed mental representations, visualization becomes a powerful tool for unlocking one's full potential and achieving peak results in various domains. Embrace visualization as a complementary practice to physical training, and watch as your performances soar to new heights, ushering you towards a path of excellence and accomplishment.

Chapter 6: Healing and Wellness through Visualization- The mind-body connection: using visualization for physical and emotional healing- Visualizing optimal health and well-being- Overcoming fears and phobias through exposure visualization- Using visualization for stress reduction and relaxation. The mind-body connection is a well-documented phenomenon, and visualization can be used as a powerful tool for healing and wellness. This chapter explores how visualization can aid in physical and emotional healing. Readers discover techniques to visualize optimal health and well-being, enabling the body's natural healing processes. Furthermore, the chapter addresses fears and phobias and introduces exposure visualization as a means of overcoming them. Lastly, it delves into stress reduction and relaxation techniques that leverage visualization for improved mental and physical well-being.

The mind-body connection is a powerful and intricate phenomenon that has been recognized for centuries. Visualization, a mental technique that uses the power of imagination, is a potent tool for promoting healing and enhancing overall wellness. This report explores the concept of healing and wellness through visualization, the scientific basis behind its effectiveness, and practical strategies for utilizing visualization to improve physical and emotional well-being.

Understanding the Mind-Body Connection:

The mind-body connection refers to the interrelationship between mental and physical health. Research has shown that our thoughts, emotions, and beliefs can influence our physiological processes, immune system, and overall health. Positive emotions, such as joy, gratitude, and love, can promote healing and strengthen the immune system, while negative emotions, like stress, anxiety, and fear, can have detrimental effects on health.

The Science Behind Healing and Wellness through Visualization:

Visualization taps into the mind-body connection by creating positive mental images that trigger emotional and physiological responses. When we visualize ourselves in a state of wellness and health, our brains interpret these images as real experiences, triggering the release of neurotransmitters and hormones that promote relaxation, reduce stress, and boost immune function.

Benefits of Healing and Wellness through Visualization:

1. Stress Reduction: Visualization can induce a relaxation response, reducing the production of stress hormones like cortisol and promoting a sense of calm and tranquility.

2. Pain Management: Visualization can be effective in managing pain by directing the mind's focus away from discomfort and fostering a sense of control over one's sensations.

3. Immune System Enhancement: Positive visualization has been associated with an increase in immune system activity, promoting the body's ability to fight off infections and illnesses.

4. Emotional Healing: Visualization can facilitate emotional healing by providing an opportunity to process

and release negative emotions, leading to improved emotional well-being.

5. Improved Coping Mechanisms: By visualizing themselves successfully overcoming challenges, individuals can build resilience and develop effective coping mechanisms for handling difficult situations.

Practical Strategies for Healing and Wellness through Visualization:

1. Relaxation Techniques: Begin your visualization practice with relaxation techniques like deep breathing or progressive muscle relaxation. A calm mind and body facilitate a more profound visualization experience.

2. Create Vivid Mental Images: Make your visualizations as detailed and vivid as possible. Engage all your senses and emotions to create a multisensory experience that feels real.

3. Focus on Specific Health Goals: Direct your visualization towards specific health goals, whether it's faster recovery from an illness, managing chronic pain, or reducing stress levels.

4. Practice Regularly: Consistency is key to reaping the benefits of visualization. Set aside dedicated time each day to engage in visualization exercises.

5. Use Guided Visualization: If you're new to visualization, guided visualization recordings or apps can provide structure and direction for your practice.

Applications of Healing and Wellness through Visualization:

1. Physical Healing: Visualize the affected areas of your body in a state of healing and well-being. See yourself recovering and regaining strength and vitality.

2. Immune System Support: Visualize your immune system as a powerful defense mechanism, effectively identifying and eliminating harmful pathogens.

3. Emotional Release: Use visualization to release emotional burdens and cultivate a sense of inner peace and emotional balance.

4. Stress Reduction: Visualize tranquil and serene environments to help your mind and body unwind and alleviate stress.

Regular practice of visualization allows us to tap into the inherent power of our minds, empowering us to take an active role in our health and wellness journey. As we continue to integrate visualization into our daily lives, we unlock the potential to achieve a state of balance, vitality, and emotional harmony, ultimately leading to a more fulfilling and enriched life.

Chapter 7: Visualization and Manifestation- The Law of Attraction: understanding the connection between visualization and manifestation- Aligning with abundance and attracting prosperity through visualization- Tips for maintaining a positive mindset and vibration- Balancing visualization with inspired action for optimal results. This focuses on the connection between visualization and the Law of Attraction, a popular belief that like attracts like. Readers gain insight into how visualization can align them with abundance, prosperity, and positive experiences. The chapter provides tips for maintaining a positive mindset and high vibration to attract the desired outcomes. It also emphasizes the importance of balancing visualization with inspired action, as visualization alone is not sufficient without taking concrete steps towards one's goals.

The mind-body connection is a powerful and intricate phenomenon that has been recognized for centuries. Visualization, a mental technique that uses the power of imagination, is a potent tool for promoting healing and enhancing overall wellness. This report explores the concept of healing and wellness through visualization, the scientific basis behind its effectiveness, and practical strategies for utilizing visualization to improve physical and emotional well-being.

Understanding the Mind-Body Connection:

The mind-body connection refers to the interrelationship between mental and physical health. Research has shown that our thoughts, emotions, and beliefs can influence our physiological processes, immune system, and overall health. Positive emotions, such as joy, gratitude, and love, can promote healing and strengthen the immune system, while negative emotions, like stress, anxiety, and fear, can have detrimental effects on health.

The Science Behind Healing and Wellness through Visualization:

Visualization taps into the mind-body connection by creating positive mental images that trigger emotional and physiological responses. When we visualize ourselves in a state of wellness and health, our brains interpret these images as real experiences, triggering the release of neurotransmitters and hormones that promote relaxation, reduce stress, and boost immune function.

Benefits of Healing and Wellness through Visualization:

1. Stress Reduction: Visualization can induce a relaxation response, reducing the production of stress hormones like cortisol and promoting a sense of calm and tranquility.

2. Pain Management: Visualization can be effective in managing pain by directing the mind's focus away from discomfort and fostering a sense of control over one's sensations.

3. Immune System Enhancement: Positive visualization has been associated with an increase in immune system activity, promoting the body's ability to fight off infections and illnesses.

4. Emotional Healing: Visualization can facilitate emotional healing by providing an opportunity to process and release negative emotions, leading to improved emotional well-being.

5. Improved Coping Mechanisms: By visualizing themselves successfully overcoming challenges, individuals can build resilience and develop effective coping mechanisms for handling difficult situations.

Practical Strategies for Healing and Wellness through Visualization:

1. Relaxation Techniques: Begin your visualization practice with relaxation techniques like deep breathing or progressive muscle relaxation. A calm mind and body facilitate a more profound visualization experience.

2. Create Vivid Mental Images: Make your visualizations as detailed and vivid as possible. Engage all your senses and emotions to create a multisensory experience that feels real.

3. Focus on Specific Health Goals: Direct your visualization towards specific health goals, whether it's faster recovery from an illness, managing chronic pain, or reducing stress levels.

4. Practice Regularly: Consistency is key to reaping the benefits of visualization. Set aside dedicated time each day to engage in visualization exercises.

5. Use Guided Visualization: If you're new to visualization, guided visualization recordings or apps can provide structure and direction for your practice.

Applications of Healing and Wellness through Visualization:

1. Physical Healing: Visualize the affected areas of your body in a state of healing and well-being. See yourself recovering and regaining strength and vitality.

2. Immune System Support: Visualize your immune system as a powerful defense mechanism, effectively identifying and eliminating harmful pathogens.

3. Emotional Release: Use visualization to release emotional burdens and cultivate a sense of inner peace and emotional balance.

4. Stress Reduction: Visualize tranquil and serene environments to help your mind and body unwind and alleviate stress.

As we continue to integrate visualization into our daily lives, we unlock the potential to achieve a state of balance, vitality, and emotional harmony, ultimately leading to a more fulfilling and enriched life.

Chapter 8: Overcoming Challenges and Obstacles- Dealing with setbacks and challenges in the visualization journey- Techniques for releasing resistance and limiting beliefs- Reinforcing resilience and perseverance through visualization- Using visualization to gain clarity during uncertain times. Overcoming Challenges and Obstacles: Strategies for Building Resilience and Achieving Success

Life is full of challenges and obstacles that test our resolve and resilience. Whether they come in the form of personal setbacks, professional hurdles, or unforeseen circumstances, overcoming challenges is an essential aspect of personal growth and success. This report delves into the art of facing and surmounting challenges, the psychological factors at play, and practical strategies to build resilience and achieve success despite adversities.

Understanding the Nature of Challenges and Obstacles:

Challenges and obstacles are part of the human experience, and they can arise in various aspects of life. They may include financial struggles, health issues, relationship conflicts, career setbacks, or pursuing ambitious goals. Challenges test our determination, resourcefulness, and adaptability, presenting opportunities for growth and learning.

The Psychological Impact of Challenges:

1. Emotional Responses: Facing challenges often elicits a range of emotions, such as fear, frustration, and self-doubt. These emotions can be overwhelming, affecting our decision-making and confidence.

2. Mindset and Perceptions: Our mindset and how we perceive challenges influence our ability to overcome them. A growth mindset, which embraces challenges as opportunities for learning and growth, can empower us to persevere.

Strategies for Overcoming Challenges and Obstacles:

1. Embrace Resilience: Resilience is the ability to bounce back from setbacks and adversity. Embracing resilience means acknowledging challenges as part of life, maintaining a positive attitude, and fostering self-belief.

2. Break Challenges into Smaller Steps: When facing significant challenges, breaking them down into smaller, manageable steps can make them less daunting. Focus on

one step at a time, celebrating each achievement along the way.

3. Seek Support and Guidance: Reach out to friends, family, mentors, or support groups when facing challenges. Discussing your struggles can provide fresh perspectives, emotional support, and practical advice.

4. Learn from Failures: Failure is a natural part of the journey to success. Embrace failures as opportunities to learn, adapt, and improve. Analyze the lessons and apply them to future endeavors.

5. Cultivate Problem-Solving Skills: Developing problem-solving skills equips us with the ability to tackle challenges creatively. Brainstorm solutions, weigh their pros and cons, and be open to trying new approaches.

6. Develop Emotional Intelligence: Emotional intelligence helps in managing emotions and stress during challenging times. Recognize your emotions, practice self-compassion, and seek healthy outlets for emotional expression.

7. Maintain a Positive Mindset: A positive mindset fosters resilience and optimism. Focus on the potential for growth and envision success despite obstacles.

Case Studies of Overcoming Challenges:

1. Athlete Overcoming Injury: A professional athlete faces a severe injury that jeopardizes their career. Through intensive rehabilitation, mental fortitude, and support from their team, they overcome the injury, returning stronger than before.

2. Entrepreneur Navigating Market Changes: An entrepreneur encounters unexpected market shifts that threaten their business. By remaining adaptable, seeking expert advice, and adjusting their business model, they steer through the challenges and thrive.

By developing problem-solving skills, emotional intelligence, and maintaining a positive mindset, individuals can build the strength and determination needed to overcome any obstacle. The case studies of athletes and entrepreneurs demonstrate the transformative power of perseverance and adaptability in the face of challenges. As we continue on our journey through life, let us embrace challenges as opportunities for growth, resilience, and self-discovery, propelling us towards a path of success and fulfillment.

Congratulations! You have completed the journey through "The Power of Visualization." Armed with this knowledge and a profound understanding of visualization's potential, you are now equipped to manifest your dreams and goals. Remember, visualization is not just a one-time exercise but a lifelong practice that can transform every aspect of your life. Embrace the power of visualization, trust the process, and watch as your visions manifest into reality. In the final chapter, we address the inevitable challenges and obstacles that may arise during the visualization journey. Readers learn strategies for dealing with setbacks and setbacks and discover techniques to release resistance and limiting beliefs that might hinder progress. The chapter emphasizes the importance of resilience and perseverance, emphasizing how visualization can reinforce these qualities. Additionally, readers gain insights into how visualization can help gain clarity and navigate uncertain times in life. By trusting the process and embracing the power of visualization, readers are reminded that they hold the key to manifesting their dreams and creating the life they desire. The conclusion leaves readers inspired and motivated to embark on their visualization journey with confidence and determination.

As you reach the closing chapters of this book, remember that the key to unlocking your true potential lies within your imagination. Embrace the power of visualization, tap into the limitless reservoir of your mind's creative prowess, and watch as your dreams manifest into reality. Harnessing your imagination is not just a fleeting notion; it is a transformative practice that can lead you to unparalleled success and fulfillment. Embrace the journey of self-discovery, set clear intentions, and fuel your visions with unwavering belief. As you navigate life's challenges, remember that the images you hold in your mind are the building blocks of your destiny. Whether you aspire to achieve career milestones, strengthen relationships, or cultivate inner peace, your imagination is the gateway to all that you desire. The journey of manifestation may not always be linear, but with perseverance and dedication, you can overcome obstacles and emerge victorious. Embrace the art of mental imagery, stay focused on your goals, and let your imagination weave the tapestry of your triumphs.You hold in your hands the keys to a world of endless possibilities. Let the wisdom of harnessing your imagination be your guiding light, illuminating the path towards a life of abundance, joy, and true success. As you turn the final page, step boldly into the realm of manifestation and watch the magic unfold. Your journey towards a life of unlimited potential starts now.

Embrace the beauty of living with intention and purpose, for it is through your imagination that you can shape your reality. As you harness the power of visualization, remember that every thought, every dream, and every desire has the potential to materialize. Cultivate a positive mindset, and let go of self-doubt and limiting beliefs that may hinder your progress. Your imagination is a boundless playground where possibilities abound. No challenge is insurmountable when you view it through the lens of creative thinking and unwavering faith in yourself. Visualize your goals as already accomplished, and let the feelings of joy and gratitude wash over you. As you nurture your visions with dedication and perseverance, you are aligning your energies with the universe, inviting success and abundance to flow into your life. Your imagination is a gift—a force that can transcend barriers and illuminate new pathways. Embrace the journey of self-discovery, for within lies the true essence of who you are and the greatness that you can achieve. Trust in your ability to manifest your dreams, and know that you possess the power to shape your destiny. As you step into the world with a renewed sense of purpose, carry with you the knowledge that your imagination is the catalyst for change. Embrace the magic of your mind, and let it guide you towards a life of meaning, joy, and fulfillment. With every thought, you are paving the way for a future filled with success beyond your wildest dreams. Your imagination is your compass; let it lead you to the extraordinary life you were always destined to live.

Happy visualizing!